DATE DUE APR 0 6

GAYLORD   PRINTED IN U.S.A.

OLIVER THE MIGHTY PIG

Jean Van Leeuwen
pictures by Ann Schweninger

DIAL BOOKS FOR YOUNG READERS
New York

For David, my Batman
And for Charles Walkes, who has a great imagination

J. V. L.

For Ron, with love

A. S.

★

Published by Dial Books for Young Readers
A division of Penguin Young Readers Group
345 Hudson Street • New York, New York 10014
Text copyright © 2004 by Jean Van Leeuwen
Pictures copyright © 2004 by Ann Schweninger
All rights reserved
Manufactured in China
The Dial Easy-to-Read logo is a registered trademark of
Dial Books for Young Readers
A division of Penguin Group (USA) Inc.
® TM 1,162,718.
1 3 5 7 9 10 8 6 4 2

Library of Congress Cataloging-in-Publication Data
Van Leeuwen, Jean.
Oliver the Mighty Pig / Jean Van Leeuwen;
pictures by Ann Schweninger.
p. cm.
Summary: Oliver feels like the superhero Mighty Pig when he wears
his Mighty Pig cape, but he finds that being a superhero
in the real world has some complications.
ISBN 0-8037-2886-7
[1. Heroes—Fiction. 2. Imagination—Fiction. 3. Play—Fiction.
4. Pigs—Fiction.] I. Schweninger, Ann, ill. II. Title.
PZ7.V3273 Omr 2004 [E]—dc21 2002007310
Reading Level 2.0

The art was created with watercolor paints
and with graphite pencil on cold-press watercolor paper

CONTENTS

THE VERY BEST PRESENT

For his birthday

Oliver got a baseball bat

and a bulldozer and a jet plane.

But his very best present

was a real genuine Mighty Pig cape.

"Oh boy!" he said. "It is just like
the one Mighty Pig wears."

Oliver tried it on.

Right away he felt different.

He was tall. And strong.

Maybe even as tall and strong as Father.

He had great big muscles

all over his body.

Oliver picked up a chair.

He picked up a table.

"Wow!" he said.

"My Mighty Pig cape works."

Maybe, thought Oliver,

I can fly too.

He climbed up on the big chair.

"Here I go," he said.

"One, two, three—fly!"

He flapped his arms and jumped.

"Ooof!"

Oliver landed right on his nose.

"Well," he said.

"Maybe my cape isn't ready to fly yet.

Maybe it is too new."

Oliver waited awhile.

After lunch he tried again.

He climbed the stairs,

all the way to the first landing.

"Okay, cape," he whispered.

"Do your stuff."

He flapped his arms as hard as he could.

And he jumped.

"Ooof!"

Oliver landed right on his stomach.

"Well," he said.

"Maybe Mighty Pig couldn't fly

right away either.

Maybe it takes practice."

At bedtime Oliver practiced on his bed.

He bounced very high.

He flapped and flapped

and flapped his arms.

"You look like a chicken," said Father.

"What are you doing?"

"I am trying to fly," said Oliver,

"like Mighty Pig."

"But Oliver," said Father.

"You know Mighty Pig is just pretend.

Like monsters are just pretend."

"Right," said Oliver.

He bounced higher.

"So when Mighty Pig flies," said Father,

"that is just pretend too."

"Right," said Oliver.

He bounced even higher.

"Did you see that?" he said.

"I think I flew a little bit that time."

"Really?" said Father.

Oliver flapped his arms

like a chicken.

"Here I come!" he cried.

"It's Mighty Pig to the rescue!"

THE BUSY DAY

"Uh-oh," said Oliver.

"There is a big car crash

on Route 88.

A zillion cars are all piled up.

This looks like a job for Mighty Pig."

Mighty Pig rushed to the rescue.

With his mighty muscles,

he lifted up the cars

and saved all the people.

"Don't thank me," he said.

"Mighty Pig is glad to help."

16

Just then he saw something else.

"Uh-oh," he said.

"A giant rocket ship up in space

is about to crash

and blow up the world.

It's another job for Mighty Pig."

Mighty Pig leaped into the sky.

With his powerful muscles,

he caught the rocket

just before it crashed.

"Whew!" he said. "That was a close one."

At lunch time, Oliver kept his cape on

just in case.

"Uh-oh," he said.

"What is it?" asked Mother.

"That bridge," said Oliver.

"It looks like it is going to collapse.

But don't worry, I will save you."

Mighty Pig jumped out of his chair.

With his muscles of steel,

he held up the bridge

until it was fixed again.

"Thanks for saving us," said Mother.

"It is all in a day's work,"

said Mighty Pig.

Outside, there was trouble.

"Uh-oh," said Oliver.

"It's the bad guys.

They have come to take over the town.

Well, we'll see about that!

Stand back, Amanda."

Mighty Pig went into action.

With his super-strong muscles,

he bumped the bad guys' heads together

and tied them up and took them to jail.

But when he got back,

Oliver saw more trouble.

"Uh-oh," he said.

"That building is on fire.

And my X-ray eyes can see

a poor little baby trapped inside."

Mighty Pig raced to the building.

With his fire-proof cape,

he ran right through the flames

and rescued the poor little baby.

"What are you doing?"

asked Amanda.

"Saving you from a burning building,"

said Mighty Pig.

"You ruined my tea party,"

said Amanda. "Go away, Oliver."

At dinner time,

Mighty Pig saved the world

from some bad guys from outer space.

At bath time, he saved a sinking ship.

Finally it was bed time.

"Well, Mighty Pig," said Mother.

"You have had a busy day."

"Yes, I have," said Oliver.

"And it may not be over yet."

"Really?" said Mother.

"I am keeping my cape handy,"

said Oliver. "Just in case."

MIGHTY PIG TO THE RESCUE

"Oliver," said Mother.

"It is time to pick up your toys."

"I can't," said Oliver.

"Mighty Pig is too busy
saving the world from
the giant buzzing bumblebees."

"Oh," said Mother.

"Well, I'm sorry to bother you."

Mighty Pig captured

all the giant buzzing bumblebees

and put them in the zoo.

"Oliver," said Mother.

"I need you to empty the wastebaskets."

"I can't," said Oliver.

"Mighty Pig is still too busy.

He is saving the world

from the awful, evil googleheads

from another planet."

"Googleheads?" said Mother.

"Their heads are like balloons,"

said Oliver.

"Well, in that case," said Mother,

"you are very busy."

Mighty Pig rounded up

the awful, evil googleheads

and sent them back to their planet.

"Oliver," said Mother.

"It is time to set the table."

"I can't," said Oliver.

"Mighty Pig is much too busy.
Now he has to save the world
from a terrible mean dragon
who is setting everything on fire."

"Oh, my," said Mother.

"You better get going."

Mighty Pig grabbed

the terrible mean dragon

and threw him into the ocean

and put out the fire.

"Mighty Pig!" called Mother.

"Help! I need you."

"Mighty Pig to the rescue!" said Oliver.

"Those giant buzzing bumblebees
ruined a whole city," said Mother.

"Just look at the cars and trucks
and falling-down houses."

"Mighty Pig will take care of that,"
said Oliver.

"Oh, and Mighty Pig," said Mother.

"I have another job for you.

The awful, evil googleheads

left their rockets behind.

They must weigh ten tons each.

Can you carry them?"

"Of course," said Mighty Pig.

"And while you are here," said Mother.

"That terrible mean dragon

blew everything off the kitchen table.

Do you think you could put it back?"

"No problem," said Mighty Pig.

"Mighty Pig," said Mother.

"You must be all tired out

from saving the world.

Would you like some juice and cookies?"

"Mighty Pig doesn't eat

juice and cookies," said Mighty Pig.

He took off his cape.

"But I do," said Oliver.

A BAD DAY

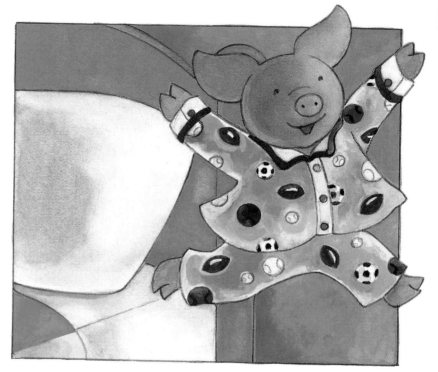

"Help! Save me!" cried someone.

Oliver jumped out of bed.

"Mighty Pig is on the way!" he said.

He reached for his cape.

But it wasn't there.

It was not on his chair.

Or on his bed. Or under his bed.

Or anywhere.

"Mother!" called Oliver.

"My Mighty Pig cape is gone."

"It is not gone," said Mother.

"It is in the wash.

Remember you spilled grape juice

on it yesterday?"

"Oh," said Oliver.

Without his Mighty Pig cape,

all of a sudden

Oliver felt small. And weak.

His muscles were like spaghetti.

"When will my cape be clean?"

he asked.

"The wash takes a while," said Mother.

"Why don't you do something else?"

"We could ride bikes," said Amanda.

"Or play checkers," said Father.

"No, thank you," said Oliver.

"I'll just wait."

Oliver sat next to the washer.

Slosh, slosh it went.

After a while the sloshing stopped.

"Is it done now?" asked Oliver.

"No," said Mother. "Now it has to rinse."

Whoosh, whoosh went the washer.

After a very long time,

the whooshing stopped.

"Now is it done?" asked Oliver.

"No," said Mother. "Now it has to dry.

I am going out to the garden."

Hummmm went the dryer.

This was taking a hundred years,

thought Oliver.

He would never get to be Mighty Pig.

Hummmm. That sounded just like the giant buzzing bumblebees.

"Uh-oh," said Oliver. "They're back."

What if he turned off the dryer

and took out his cape?

He didn't care if it was still wet.

But what would Mother say?

She would be angry.

She might take away his cape.

But he needed it right now.

The world was waiting to be saved

from the giant buzzing bumblebees.

Oliver climbed onto his stool.

He reached up.

"Look at the pretty flowers
I picked," said Mother.

Oliver climbed down from his stool.

"Is it done yet?" he asked.

"No," said Mother. "But soon."

Oliver sat next to the dryer

for a hundred years.

Until, finally, it stopped.

"Here is your cape," said Mother.

"Nice and clean."

Oliver put it on.

Right away he felt different.

Much taller. A lot stronger.

And his great big muscles were back.

"Those giant buzzing bumblebees
are loose again," said Oliver.
"I have to go.
It's Mighty Pig to the rescue!"
Maybe, he thought, he could even fly.